LOWRIDERS to the CENTER of the EARTH

BOOK 2

By CATHY CAMPER
Illustrated by RAÚL THE THIRD

chronicle books · san francisco

ELIRIO MALARIA, LUPE IMPALA, AND EL CHAVO FLAPJACK OCTOPUS HAD THEIR OWN GARAGE. PLUS THEY HAD THE MOST MECHANICALLY INVENTIVE, EXQUISITELY DETAILED CAR IN THE UNIVERSE, WITH POWERS GLEANED FROM THE GALAXY!
PLAZA
OPEN
Flappy, can you buff out that sedan?
Sure thing!

RIDERS
IN
Bajito y Suavecito
all day ⟷ cada dia
ELIRIO
CHAVO
FLAPJACK
OCTOPUS
NOPAL
R3
I love having our *own* place!
Time to get to work on that van.

LUPE WAS A MASTER MECHANIC, AN IMPALA EXTRAORDINAIRE! WITH A WRENCH AND A RATCHET, SHE COULD REPAIR ANYTHING.
RUTA
Amor y Cohetes

FLAPPY WAS A WASHCLOTH-WIELDING DYNAMO, PURO PODER* TIMES EIGHT!
NOA! NOA! NOA!
NOA
NOA
FJ
JUANGA
Bright eyes
Kooky

ELIRIO PAINTED WITH HIS BILL. HIS BEAK WAS AS STEADY AS A SURGEON'S HAND, HIS SKILL IN DETAILING CARS UNPARALLELED.
Elirio Malaria

* PURE POWER

QUAKE
CRUMBLE
RÚMBLE ~ RUMBLE.
HEY! Who's shaking the car?
TSUNAMI?!
Another earthquake, vatos!!*
¡Un terremoto!** What about our car?
YIKES!
* DUDES ** AN EARTHQUAKE!

IT'S FALLING!
Edificio
Bajito y Suavecito
all day cadadia
LUPE IMPALA
ELIRIO
MALARIA
EL CHAVO

Not if I can help it!
Go Flappy!

She's too heavy!
THUMP
I'll fly 'er down!
THUMP

¡Ándale!*

YES!
FWOOOSH!!!

LUCKILY, THEIR CAR'S HYDRAULICS MEANT IT HIPPED AND HOPPED . . .
DAILY CHISME
Bajito y Suavecito
all day cada dia
DAILY CHISME
AND DIPPED AND DROPPED. NO PROBLEM!

* COME ON!

* GARAGE ** CRAZY

PAT PAT PAT PAT PAT PAT
PURR
PURR
PURR
GATO
VASO
INK
I need Genie to knead tortillas on my tummy until I fall asleep!
It's lonely when I'm painting in the shop without los soniditos de mi amigo.*
He loves it when I sing to him.
CLANG!!
WE NEED GENIE!
* MY FRIEND'S LITTLE SOUNDS, PURRS

LOST CAT

Genie

FRIENDLY—ORANGE—LARGE—
LIKES TO TAKE NAPS

Contact Lowriders in Space if you find him

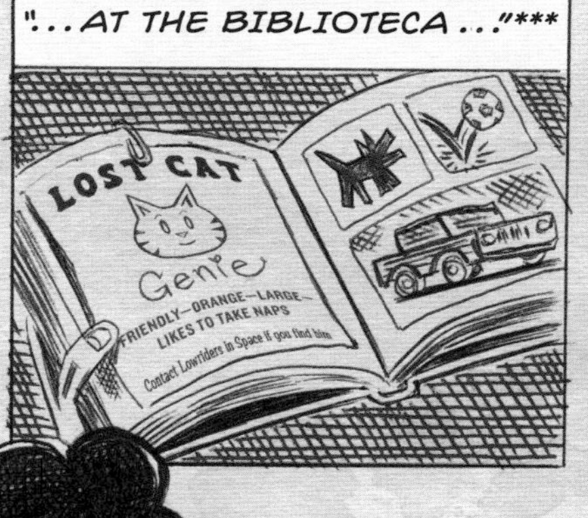

* NEIGHBORHOOD **MARKET ***LIBRARY ****MILK CARTONS

No one's called.
Does this old thing even work?
LUPE

HELP MEE-EEEEW
That echo was weird!
It sounded like a cry for help!
What if that's Genie? What if he's in trouble?
FORTUNA
224
LOST CAT
Genie
FRIENDLY—ORANGE—LARGE—
LIKES TO TAKE NAPS
LOST CAT
Genie
LOST CAT

El Chavo, you have to pick things that fit in your suitcase.

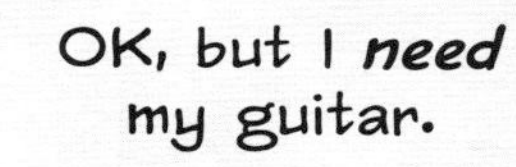

* CAT **MY BOOKS ***MY TOYS

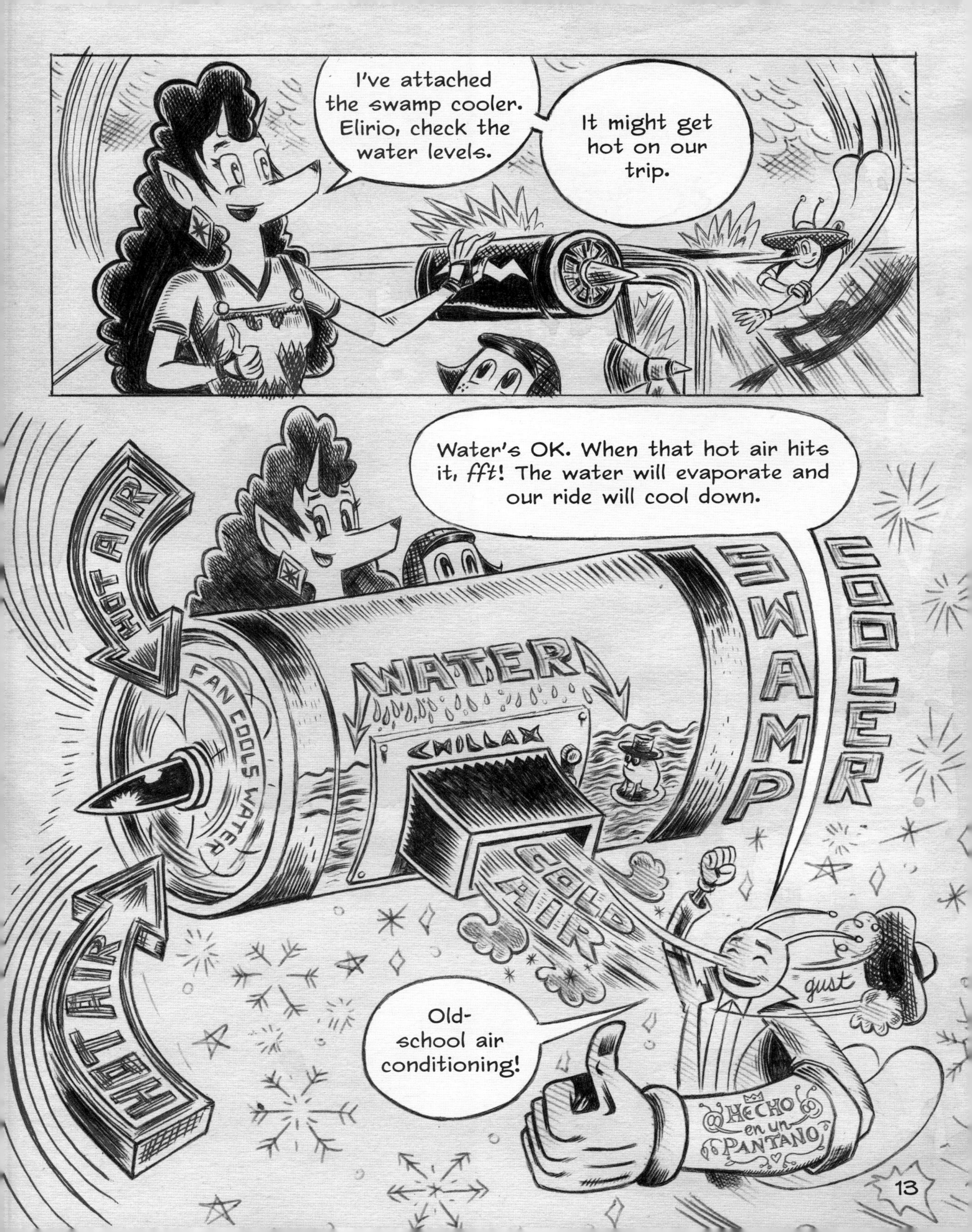
I've attached the swamp cooler. Elirio, check the water levels.
It might get hot on our trip.
Water's OK. When that hot air hits it, *fft*! The water will evaporate and our ride will cool down.
HOT AIR
FAN COOLS WATER
WATER
CHILLAX
SWAMP COOLER
COLD AIR
HOT AIR
gust
Old-school air conditioning!
HECHO en un PANTANO

¡Vámonos!* We have to follow those footprints.
ROPA POR LIBRA
I'll follow the tracks, you follow me.
"TOO BAD OUR SPEAKER'S BUSTED. OUR RIDE COULD USE SOME TUNES."
ALTAVOZ
I'll play some cruising music instead.
CLANG
TWANG!
SCREECH!
* LET'S GO!

GE-NIE! GE-NIE!
Wow, Genie's gone farther than I thought.
140
OK!
GAS GUZZLER
POMADA de la LIBERTY BELL
VERA la CALAVERA
CALDO de

"LOOKS LIKE HE STOPPED FOR SOMETHING TO EAT . . ."
POLLO del MAR
TUNA

". . . AND SOMETHING TO DRINK . . ."
JIMENEZ

". . . BUT HE KEPT ON GOING! GENIE LEFT TOWN!"
EL GRAN SAPO
Here, kitty kitty!
HOLA
ARRIBA
WE DELIVER
YOU ARE LEAVING!
LOST CAT
LOST CAT

LATER . . .
. . . a la playa,*
to the shore . . .

RORR

What was that?

. . . lying in the sun, on my towel . . .

That sounded mean!

Wait, slow down, Lupe! We're headed straight for a cornfield.

* TO THE BEACH

¿¡Maíz gigante?!*
That's some BIG corn on the cob!
SScreech!**
Genie's tracks keep going . . .
Why would Genie go in there?
¡elote!** ¡squawk!
Are those crows talking to us?
¡coyote!
PELIGRO
¡NUNCA MÁS!***
* GIANT CORN?! ** CORNCOB! *** NEVER MORE!

* TO THE LEFT OR THE RIGHT?

Now which way?
I'm confused.
I think we're lost.
HELP!
HELLO?
GO!
That voice is creeping me out!

Who me? Elementary, homes,** I'm no trickster, I'm just punny, heh heh heh.

* YES, THANK YOU! ** SHORT FOR HOMEBOY, SOMETHING YOU CALL A FRIEND
*** MISTER **** MISTER CAT; BUT ALSO A PUN: "SEEN YOUR CAT?"
***** HA HA HA! ****** (IN RESPONSE TO A PUN) HOW DUMB!

* *GIVE ME MY HAT, STUPID CHICKEN!*

MICTLANTECUHTLI
"MICTLANTECUHTLI, THE AZTEC GOD OF THE UNDERWORLD, LOVES TO WRESTLE, AND HE LOVES TO SHOW OFF. HE STARTED OFF WRESTLING THE SKELETONS HE RULED OVER, FIRST SMALL ONES, LIKE MONKEYS, THEN BIGGER ONES, LIKE ALLIGATORS."
¡Yo soy el mero mero!*
M
DIENTE
* I AM THE ONE AND ONLY!

* HOLLOW BONES!

"HE CAME UP TO EARTH AND CHALLENGED XILONEN, THE AZTEC GODDESS OF CORN."
An ojo* for an ojo, bully!
Then again, with all your eyes, maybe not . . .
You're on, Cornflakes!
"XILONEN WAS ATHLETIC AND STRONG."
SWOOSH!!
ACK!
"THEY WRESTLED FROM DAWN–"
BAM
* EYE

"–UNTIL DUSK,"

"DOWN INTO THE UNDERWORLD."

"BUT THE HEAT OF THE UNDER-WORLD POPPED XILONEN'S CORN, CONFUSING HER."
POP
POP
POP
You lose, Cracker Jack!
Nincom-poop!

"MICTLANTECUHTLI FORCED HER TO BUILD THIS MAZE."
¡Pronto,* popcorn! I don't have all day!
"HE TRAPS CREATURES IN THE MAZE, CAPTURES THEM, AND FORCES THEM TO INHABIT MICTLAN, THE UNDERWORLD, WHERE THEY LIVE ON AS SKELETONS."

* HURRY

But why would he take Genie?
Who knows? Maybe he has a crisis with mices. ¡Je je je!*
But you don't want to mess with Mic. He's big and mean, he collects bones, and he's always looking for more.
If he has Genie, we need to find him! Will you take us?
You've *gato* be *kitten* me! Go to the underworld? I can lead you through the maze, but once you get to Mictlan, you're on your own.
elote
con
chile
limon
CLUCK!
CLUCK!
Follow me.
SNIFF
SNIFF

* HEH HEH HEH!

* OCTOPUS GUY ** WHAT DO FISH DO? *** NOTHING!; BUT ALSO A PUN: "SWIM"

Here we are! To get to the underworld, cross the railroad tracks, go through a field of boulders, and follow the road to el volcán.*
The bats will show you the way.
Thanks for your help.
De nada.** I hope you have a purr-fect trip.
Oh, and if you find some huesos along the way, you might be able to trade them for your cat. Jes' sayin' . . .
* THE VOLCANO ** IT'S NOTHING; YOU'RE WELCOME

Wait—one more thing. Which road goes to the volcano?

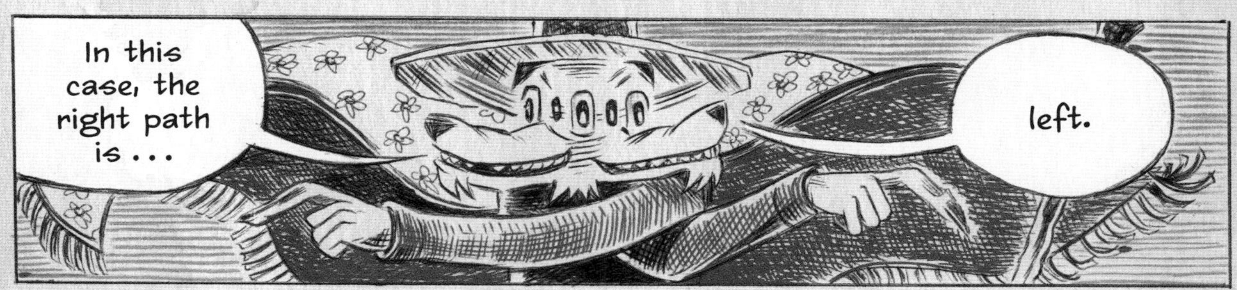
In this case, the right path is . . .
left.

Does he mean the right is left behind because left is right . . . ?
Or left is wrong . . .
so that means the right is left for us to take?
Don't worry guys. We'll just drive toward the volcano.

CRUZ
Railroad tracks! So far, so good!
BUMP BUMP

Those giant heads were carved from boulders the volcano spit out.

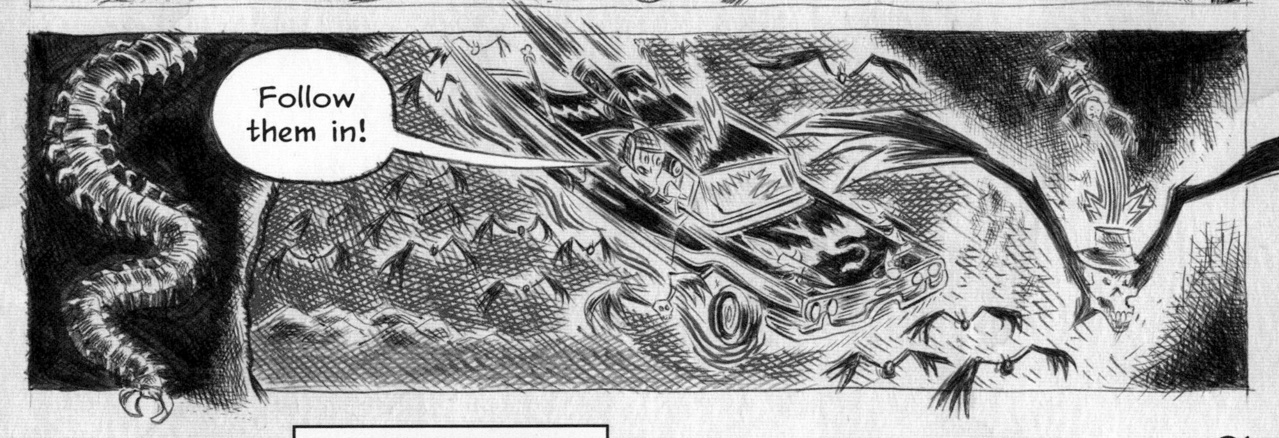

* "FOLLOW THE BATS"

It's pitch-black in here! Turn on the meteor headlights and fire the comet exhaust.
Hit the underlighting!
AHHH!
¡Miren todos los tesoros!*
NOSE
* LOOK AT ALL THE TREASURES!

Diente
podrido
III
Raul the Third

* MURALS ** MY HOUSE

Whoa! Hey, something is pulling me!
VVVVVVVRRRRRMMMM

OOOFFF!
THUNK

Lodestone! A magnet to fix our busted speaker!

It weighs a ton!

Now we can listen to heavy rock!

I'll just slip the lodestone behind the voice coil, and we'll be all set.

Sedimentary
Oooo! Sedentary rocks . . . like napping at the beach . . . ZZZ . . .
¡Despiértate,* Flappy! That rock is solidified sand!
METAMORPHIC
And here are some metaphoric rocks—these are the building blocks of poets everywhere!
Vato, your words are mixed up CRAZY!

* WAKE UP

These rocks got squeezed by the Earth and became new kinds of rocks.

You're so smart, Elirio. How come you know so much?
FJ
I collected palabras* when I was small. I put the ones I liked in my paintings.
* WORDS

WAAAAAAAA!
Hey guys, listen. Do you hear that?
WAAAAAA
WAAAAAA

* WHERE ARE MY BABIES? ** CHILDREN *** MY CHILDREN

Hey, it's OK.
WAA! WAA! WAA! WAA!

Can it be?
My baby?

After so much searching, I've found you, my sweet one!
Although I don't remember you having so many legs . . .

¡Mi chiquito!*
I am NOT a baby!

Bueno,** El Chavo Flapjack, she likes you, you calmed her down.
Good thing. My ears were hurting.

* MY BABY! ** GOOD

** BUCKET ** TEARS *** A MONSTER, LIKE THE BOOGEYMAN, THAT PARENTS USE TO SCARE THEIR KIDS INTO BEHAVING*

YEEII!
Lupe, stop!
It's El Cucuy, he's after me!

What? Where is he?

WAAA!
AUUGH!!

Homes, it's just El Chavo hiding.
Flappy, back in the car. Now!
This cave is playing tricks on me.
I'm gonna escape under the seat!
¿DÓNDE ESTÁ MI HIJO?*
* WHERE IS MY SON?

The car is filling up with tears!
What's going on up there?
¡SOCORRO!
Flappy, socorro!*
Make her stop crying!
* HELP

Oh no! ¡Mis amigos!* They can't breathe.
LOST CAT
Genie
But to stop the tears means . . .
LAGRIMAS
BORBUJAS
* MY FRIENDS!

. . . arrrgh! I have to be a baby again!
Can someone open a window?
Chale,* that was a close one!
SPLOOSH!
OOSH!
LET'S GET OUTTA HERE!
* DANG, NO WAY

This is a steep drop!
HOT!
ZONE
DRINK AGUA
¡QUE CALOR!
DIABLITO
SAPO
Hey look, a drive-in! Maybe we should stop and eat.
¡Tortas, tortas, tortas!*
TORTAS NICO
¡QUÉ RICO, LAS TORTAS NICO!
MILANESA LENGUA TRIPITAS
MURCIELAGO
TACO TODA
COMIDA COURT
* SANDWICHES

* A DOG-LIKE MONSTER WITH RED EYES, THOUGHT TO SUCK THE BLOOD OF GOATS AND OTHER LIVESTOCK.

* WOW, BROTHER, OR WOW, MAN ** GOAT'S BLOOD!

Mmm, yum!
I swear I smell impala!
CHUEY
Hmmm.
I don't remember seeing that on the menu . . .
CHUEY CHUPAS
We gotta get out of here rápido!*
Flappy, turn off all the lights.
Elirio, drop the car. We need to go . . .
LIGHT
HEAVY
LOW and SLOW
CHUEY CHUPAS
CHUEY CHUPAS
* FAST

I gotta do something. I'll be right back.

CHUEY CHUPAS
CHUEY CHUPAS
RUMBLE
Shhh . . .

FFSSSSS

Huh?
Don't worry, Lupe, he can't follow us now.
I let the air out of his tires.
VROOOOM!

We're bajito y suavecito,* but he's high and dry!
Phew! That was close. Let's scram.
AARRRRGGGHHH!
¿Quién ponchó mis llantas?**
* LOW AND SLOW ** WHO PUNCTURED MY TIRES?

Wow, the breeze is really warm!
HOT HOT HOT
LEAVING EARTH'S MANTLE
Welcome to the OUTER CORE
TOMA MUCHA AGUA
Fwoosh

My hair is going mental!

We'll change your nappy when we get there.

Lupe, watch the road!
I can't see! My hair is in the way!
Screech!

MICTLAN REALM OF THE DEAD
enter
KRACK
VROOM!
Look out!
ARF!
RAUL 3RD

ente
Oops!
PHEW!!
Phew! The car's OK.
But we'll have to clean up these bones.
SHOVE
Maybe I can reassemble them.
Uh Lupe, that's not quite right.
enter
I hope Mic-lecty-tecty-cootly, I mean, Miclanty-tanty-cootybooty, *whatever*-his-name-is, doesn't get too angry.

WHAT DID YOU CALL ME?
OF THE

I'm Mic to you, ¡idiotas!* If you mispronounce my name one more time, I'll pop out your eyeballs and add them to my necklaces!
Just what do you think you're doing down here?
* IDIOTS!

Oh, hello, señor! We lost our cat, Genie. Coyote thought he might have ended up down here. Have you seen a big orange cat?
We heard you like bones. I made you this bowtie. We . . . we . . . th-thought we could t-trade it for our cat.

What would I want with your puny rearrangement of MY bones?
HEY VATO QUE PASU?
I'm Lord of the Underworld! I've got all the skeletons I want! Just not yours . . .
SNAP

YET!

KRACK
¡Socorro!

Hey Pancakes! How do you keep track of all them legs?
That's not my name!
Arf!
REX

Hey Pancakes, howza 'bout I flip your stacks?
FLIP
CHILE TODAY
HOT TAMALE

HUEVOS
Don't call me that!

LEAVE FLAPPY ALONE!
Now where's our cat?

We *KNOW* you have him!
Genie's ours, you can't just take him!

FOOLS! I have your gatito* all right. If you want your kitty cat, you'll have to go get him first. He's right over . . .
THERE!

What is *that*?

* KITTEN

IT'S THE WIND OF KNIVES
Mew!
SLICE
¡JA JA JA!
It's the Wind of Knives! When people die, that wind strips their flesh away so they can live with me as skeletons in Mictlan. If you want your cat, you'll have to GO THROUGH TO THE OTHER SIDE.
SNAP

* HAM ** BRAVE *** ALL RIGHT

But will our car protect us?
Hmmm.

Guys, guys I've got it! ¡Vámonos!
Elirio, you take the wheel. Flappy, you're on the gas pedals and gear shift.

I'll use this!
Our speaker?
Lupe, are you loca? Those knives are gonna cut us up like calamari!

Think about it guys, think! What are knives made of? And how did we just fix our speaker?

MAGNET!

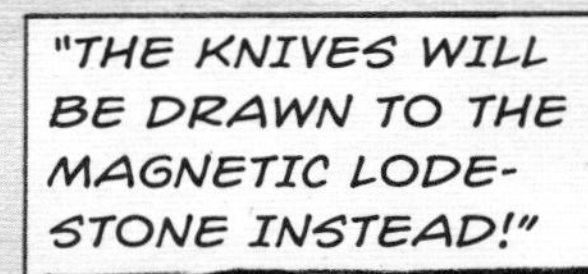
"THE KNIVES WILL BE DRAWN TO THE MAGNETIC LODE-STONE INSTEAD!"

Lupe, why did we ever doubt you?

Don't fall!
Just keep her steady and I'll do the rest.
ZEKE

Ay, Lupe, ten cuidado por favor.*
Easy on the gas, Chavo . . .
Closer!
¡JA JA JA JA JA JA JA JA JA JA!
* BE CAREFUL PLEASE

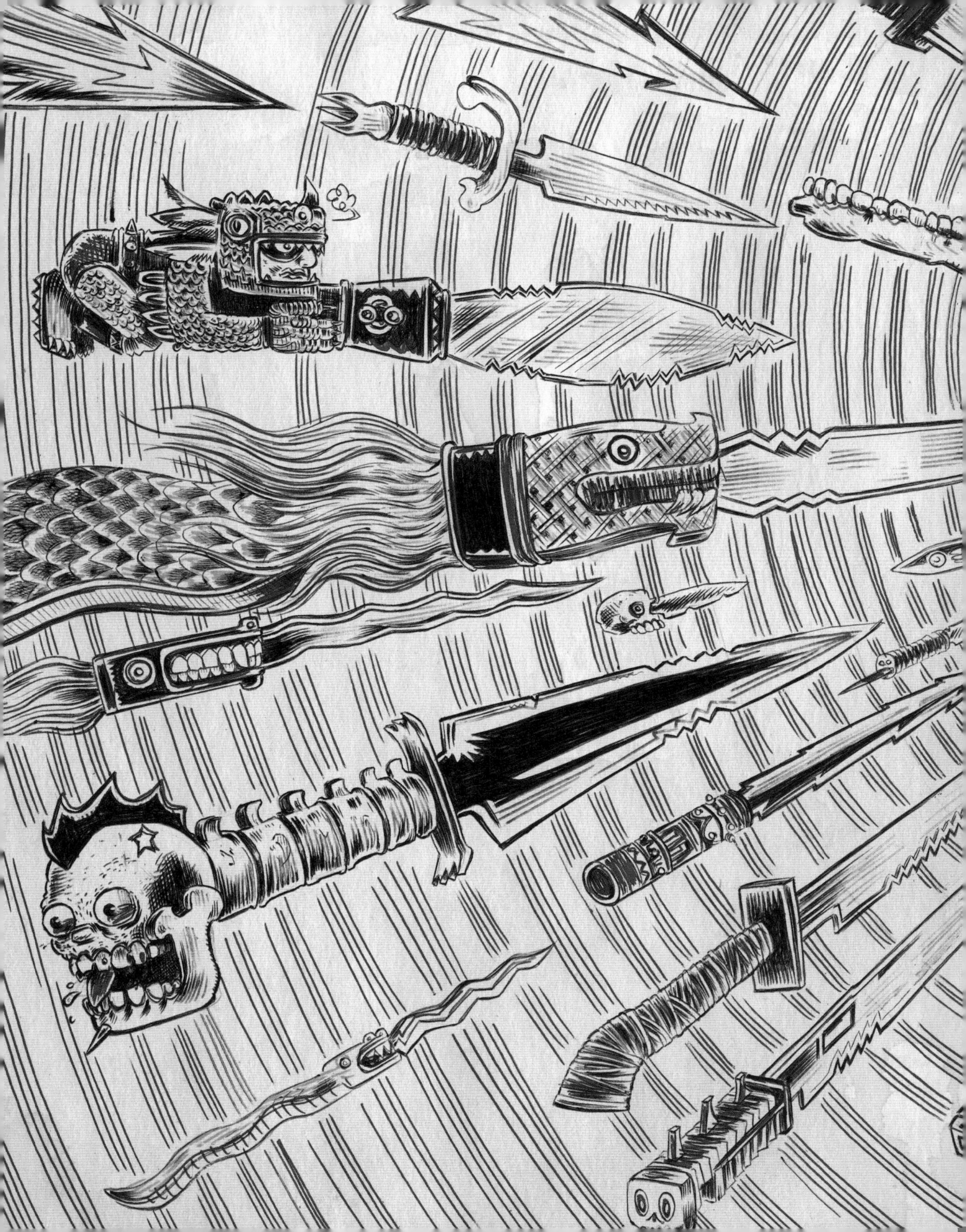

¡Imposible!* The knives are sticking to that hunk of junk?
* IMPOSSIBLE!

Elirio, steer away from the cage.
KA-CHING!!
Flapjack, grab Genie!

Meow!

BUZZZ
ALTAVOZ
Elirio, cut the power so the electromagnetic coil will drop the knives.
They're falling like dead moscas!*
KLANG!
KLANG!
Except for this one. It's stuck!
ALTAVO
An Aztec obsidian blade. Maybe ancient powers put it there, just like the sword in the stone!
ALTAV
Look who I found.

* FLIES

* WHAT'S HAPPENED TO YOU? ** WITH *** SPEAKER

* FRIEND ** LITTLE CAKE, PANCAKE *** DEEP-FRIED BURRITOS
**** THE CENTER OF THE PLANET

* OH NO, MY SON! ** THAT HEAT!

Yikes! It's even hot on Pluto!
caliente!!
¡orno!
I think we're stuck.
FRENO
BLARP!
My water's evaporating! Hurry! I feel like octopus jerky!
SSS

* BABY ** SHELLFISH IN SOUP

FLAPPY!
Drive, Lupe, drive!
I'm trying! I got the pedal to the floor! Elirio, flip the switches!
Let's get these tires hopping!
C'mon, c'mon!!
¡Así mero!* Our hydraulics are making the car hip and hop, dip and drop, lowrider style!
And it's working. The tires are freeing up.
* JUST LIKE THAT!

CENTRO
MACETA
OJO
¡YO SOY
EL CENTRO!*
* I AM THE CENTER!

CALIENTE
Hold on, El Chavo Flapjack!
There's only one gota* left.
FJ
* DROP

¿Mi'jo?*
One gota...
PLINK
We made it!
... Flappy?
My baby! I've lost you again!
* MY SON (CONTRACTION)

WAAAAAAA!!
¡Mi Hijo! ¡Mi Hijo!

Whaa happened? Did we make it?

Mi'jo, you've come back!
Homes, thank goodness you're OK! You were looking a bit seco.* Now your bucket is filled up!
¡LÁGRIMAS!
Ahhh . . . salt water!

* DRY

If Flappy's OK, let's get outta this horno* and get this water back to Mic!

BROOOMM!!
Genie here we come!
What about me?

* OVEN

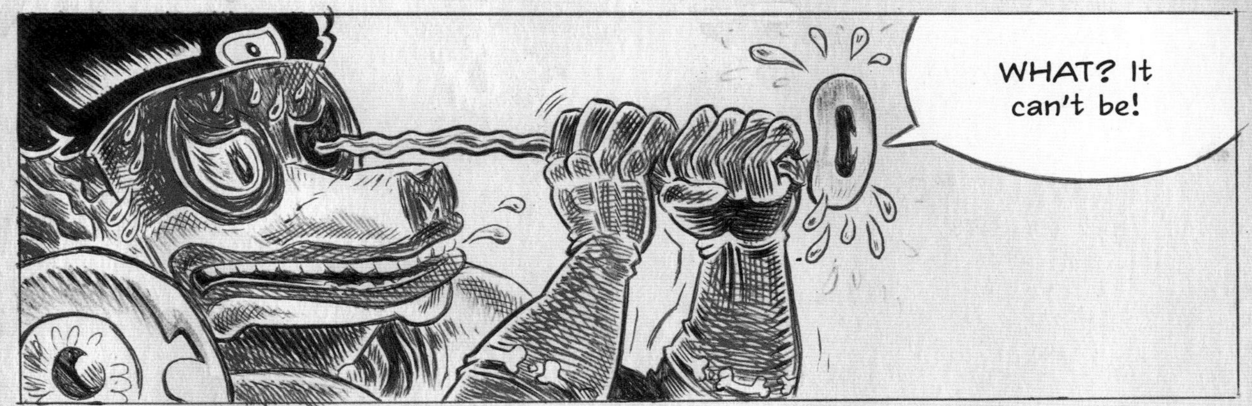
WHAT? It can't be!

Impossible!
Mic-tlan-ti-poopy looks mad!

We're back with your stupid bucket! Now give us our cat!

NO ONE OUT-SMARTS
MICTLANTECUHTLI!
NO ONE!
Especially not chamacos* like you!
* PIP-SQUEAKS

Gimme that!
Our car key!

Without it we're trapped!

¡Exacto!* And now, I'm gonna teach you all a lesson!

I think we'll decide this one . . .
PUSH!

* EXACTLY!

FJ
SOY GATO
MICTLANTEC
PALOMITA

...IN THE RING!
CAMPEON de los MUERTOS
REY de los HUESOS
MASCARAS
PALOMITAS
SPLAT!
PARKING 10 BONES
DING-DING!

"IN THIS CORNER, REPRESENTING THE UNDERWORLD AND ALL THE SKELETONS IN THE UNIVERSE . . ."
. . . MICTLANTECUHTLI!
MIC
¡El rudo!*
* IN WRESTLING, THE BAD GUY OR BRAWLER

* OF THE SEA ** IN WRESTLING, THE GOOD GUYS *** DON'T WORRY

Don't make me laugh, you donut hole!
You'll be crying once you feel my cannonball!

OOOF!

You look like a soggy, saggy diaper.
BOUNCE!

Yepa!
Yepa!
Yepa!
PUNT!
Mictlantecuhtli shoots and . . .
Spritz!
window cleaner
¡GOL!*
Round one goes to Mictlantecuhtli! Up next, Lupe Impala.
Whew! My head is spinning!
* GOAL!

speed
125 lbs

Running, plus my weight, plus bouncing off the rope at just the right angle equals ¡TRIUNFO!*

Oh no!
BOOM!
BOOM!
BOOM!

Giddy up, Impala!

FLIP!
MIC

* TRIUMPH!

* RUBBER BAND ** WHO'S NEXT?

And finally, we have Elirio Malaria, a tiny insecto.*
Now it's all on me.
Good thing I wore my lucky chili pepper choners!**
¡MÁSCARA CONTRA CABELLERA!***
But I don't even *have* hair!
MÁSCARA CONTRA ANTENNAE!****
DING! DING!
Meet La Manopla!*****
* INSECT ** UNDERPANTS *** MASK VS. HAIR! **** MASK VS. ANTENNAE!
***** A WRESTLING MOVE FROM THE DOMINICAN REPUBLIC

I may be tiny.
BLAM!
Huh?
But my beak is the fastest brush around!
JA! JA! JA! JA! JA!
Free tatuajes?*
I can live with that!
* TATTOOS

* BUTT ** A LICENSE PLATE; SLANG FOR A TATTOO ON THE LOWER BACK *** SPANKING

NOW!
WHO WANTS TO WATCH ME TURN THIS CAT INTO A SKELETON?
CAN YOU DIG IT?
ACE
We have to rescue Genie before it's too late.
¿Pero cómo?*
We'll have to work together.

* BUT HOW?

Here, kitty kitty. Don't worry, I'll get my best people to polish your bones.
No dude, a la derecha!

I knew that blade would come in handy. Chavo, stretch one of your tentacles down to the car.

LIBRE

ALTAVOZ

We need to cut the rope holding the cage.
Sí.

* SPARKS! USED HERE AS AN EXCLAMATION
** WHAT'S GOING ON HERE?

* GIRL ** FARTS *** MY EYES!

It's bath time, Mic-lan-ti-panty stinky!
DRENCH
Nobody messes with my pelo!*
Oh no you don't! Leave—Flappy—
* HAIR

-ALONE!
JABON
Great shot, Lupe!
Genie's glowing!

HE'S TRANS-
FORMING!
ROAR

I AM TEPEYOLLOTL, THE JAGUAR OF NIGHT, LORD OF ANIMALS, DARKENED CAVES, ECHOES, AND EARTHQUAKES, AND I'VE COME TO RECLAIM MY POWER!!
How DARE you steal my power of echo and scare my friends?
Genie *talks?*

* DON'T BE RIDICULOUS! ** PUNKS

OH NO YOU WON'T!
RIIIIIP!

My curls! My mask!!

* LIKE A BOWLING BALL. ** PARTY!

* DAY OF THE DEAD

LUPE IMPALA★ELIRIO MALARIA★EL CHAVO
FLAPJACK OCTOPUS
These skeletons know how to party!
They even have musicans!
bigote
YAY!
LOWRIDERS in SPACE
RAUL the Third
CATHY CAMPER

** AY YA YA YAY SING AND DON'T CRY! A LINE FROM THE POPULAR SONG "CIELITO LINDO." ** I AM LIKE THE GREEN CHILE, LLORONA, SPICY BUT TASTY. A LINE FROM THE FOLK SONG "LA LLORONA."*

* WELL, THE VOLCANO ** LOWRIDER *** FAMILY

* I LOVE YOU SO MUCH.

SPIN
FIESTA
Nobody honors the dead like the dead.
LOWRIDERS IN SPACE GANA
TAP TAPPITY TAP!!
RANCHERITAS

ooo!
ooo!
RUEDA DE LA FORTUNA
SMILE
Ferris
¡elotes! ¡con chile y limón!
elotes
TOOT TOOT!

* WHAT BEAUTIFUL MUSIC!

This sound system is fantastic.
uerida
querida
frijoles pintos
en mi tortilla
It's our new speaker!
Great song! Who's singing, Flappy?

It's me!
That proves it! This speaker **must** be fantastic if it makes even **you** sound this good!

I miss cruising the skies with you guys. So for now . . .
Meow!
. . . I'd just like to be your big orange cat.
Genie, you're a superhero!

We made it to the center of the Earth and back.

How 'bout a couple loops around the galaxy before we head home?
Cruise to the stars!
cuate
cohete

"BAJITO Y SUAVECITO,
UP AND OUT. BLAST OFF!
BECAUSE-WE'RE-"
LOWRIDERS
IN SPACE!

What Does it Mean / ¿Que significa?

¿A la izquierda o la derecha?—To the left or the right?

a la playa—to the beach

amiga/amigo—friend

¡Ándale!—Come on!

¡Así mero!—Just like that!

¡Ay no, mi hijo!—Oh no, my son!

¡Ay ya ya yay canta y no llores!—Ay ya ya yay sing and don't cry! A line from the popular song "Cielito Lindo."

bajito y suavecito—low and slow

barrio—neighborhood

bebé—baby

biblioteca—library

bocina—speaker

bueno—good

cartones de leche—milk cartons

chale—dang, no way

chamacos—pip-squeaks

chica—girl

chimichangas—deep-fried burritos

¡Chispitas!—Sparks!, used as an exclamation

choners—underpants

Chupacabra [chew-puh-CAW-bra]—Also known as the goat sucker, the chupacabra is a dog-like monster with red eyes, known throughout Central and South America and the Caribbean for attacking cattle and livestock.

cola—butt

como una pelota de boliche—like a bowling ball

con—with

cubeta—bucket

¡Dame mi sombrero, stupid pollo!—Give me my hat, stupid chicken!

de nada—it's nothing; you're welcome

del mar—of the sea

despiértate—wake up

Día de los Muertos—Day of the Dead

¿Dónde está mi hijo?—Where is my son?

¿Dónde están mis bebés?—Where are my babies?

el centro del planeta—the center of the planet

El Chavo Pulpo—Octopus Guy

El Cucuy [el coo-COO-ee]—a monster, like the boogeyman, that parents use to scare their kids into behaving; the monster that hides under your bed

el rudo—literally, the rude one; in wrestling, the bad guy or brawler

el volcán—the volcano

¡Elote!—Corncob!

¡Exacto!—Exactly!

exoskeleton—on insects, a tough outer shell like armor that protects them

familia—family

gatito—kitten

gato—cat

¡GOL!—GOAL!

gota—drop

híjole, 'mano—wow, brother or wow, man

homes—short for homeboy, something you call a friend

horno—oven

hueco—hollow

Huehuecoyotl [way-way-coh-YO-tul]—the Aztec trickster coyote god

huesos—bones

¡Idiotas!—Idiots!

igneous rock—rock formed by hardened lava and magma, often associated with volcanoes

¡Imposible!—Impossible!

insecto—insect

¡Ja ja ja!—Ha ha ha!

jamón—ham

¡Je je je!—Heh heh heh!

La Llorona [la yo-RO-na]—a ghostly woman fated to search for her dead children forever, crying loudly wherever she goes

La Manopla—literally, the mitten; in Luche Libre in the Dominican Republic, a wrestling move; also, cheating by using brass knuckles

lágrimas—tears

liga—rubber band

loca/loco—crazy

lodestone—a kind of mineral that's naturally magnetic

los soniditos de mi amigo—my friend's little sounds, purrs

los técnicos—literally, the technicians; in wrestling, the good guys

Lucha Libre—professional wrestling in Mexico and other countries in Central and South America and the Caribbean

magma—molten rock

¡¿Maíz gigante?!—Giant corn?!

marisco in sopa—shellfish in soup

¡Máscara contra antennae!—Mask versus antennae!

¡Máscara contra cabellera!—literally, mask versus hair; in Lucha Libre, a masked wrestler versus one with hair instead of a mask

mercado—market, store

metamorphic rocks—rocks that changed into their current form because of intense pressure in the Earth

mi casa—my house

¡Mi chiquito!—My baby!

mi hijo/mi'jo—my son

Mictlantecuhtli [mick-lan-te-COOT-lee]—Aztec god of the underworld, who rules over all that die of natural causes. The Aztecs believed that a wind of knives ripped off the skin of the dead, who then lived with him as skeletons.

¡Miren todos los tesoros!—Look at all the treasures!

¡Mis amigos!—My friends!

mis libros—my books

mis juguetes—my toys

¡Mis niños!—My children!

¡Mis ojos!—My eyes!

moscas—flies

murales—murals

nalgada—spanking

niños—children

¡No seas ridículo!—Don't be ridiculous!

no te preocupes—don't worry

¡Nunca más!—Never more!

obsidian—a volcanic glass formed when lava cools rapidly, which was used by the Aztecs for arrows, knives, and other tools

ojo—eye

órale—all right

¡Pachanga!—Party!

pachucos—punks

palabras—words

pedos—farts

pelo—hair

¿Pero cómo?—But how?

pronto—hurry

pues—well

puro poder—pure power

¡Qué bárbaro!—An expression in response to a bad pun, like in English, someone would say "How awful!" or "How dumb!"

¡Qué calor!—That heat!

¡Qué chido!—Cool!

¿Qué hace el pez? ¡Nada!—A pun: What do fish do? Nothing! (The word nada means "nothing" but it also means "swim.")

¡Qué linda música!—What beautiful music!

¿Qué pasa aquí?—What's going on here?

¿Qué te pasó?—What's happened to you?

¿Quién ponchó mis llantas?—Who punctured my tires?

¿Quién sigue?—Who's next?

ranfla—lowrider

rápido—fast

¡Sangre de cabra!—Goat's blood!

seco—dry

sedimentary rocks—rocks formed by hardened sand and mud, often at the bottom of oceans, rivers, or other bodies of water

señor—mister

Señor gato—A pun: In Spanish it means "Mister cat," but in English it sounds like you're saying: Seen your cat?

¡Sí, gracias!—Yes, thank you!

sigan los murciélagos—follow the bats

socorro—help

stalactite—pointed piece of rock that hangs from the roof of a cave, formed by mineral-rich water dripping over many years

swamp cooler—an old fashioned type of cooler used in cars that allows hot air to flow over water to cool the air

taller—garage

tatuajes—tattoos

te quiero mucho—I love you so much

ten cuidado por favor—be careful please

Tepeyollotl [teh-puh-yo-LOT-ull]—the Aztec Jaguar god, who rules over animals, darkened caves, echoes, and earthquakes

tortas—sandwiches

tortita—little cake, pancake

¡Triunfo!—Triumph!

¡Un terremoto!—An earthquake!

una placa—a plate, in this case, a license plate. Tattoos on the lower back are sometimes referred to as license plates.

valiente—brave

¡Vámonos!—Let's go!

vato/vatos—dude, guy/dudes, guys

Xilonen [shel-OH-nen]—the youthful Aztec goddess of corn and fertility

Yo soy como el chile verde, Llorona Picante pero sabroso—I am like the green chile, Llorona, spicy but tasty. A line from the folk song "La Llorona."

¡Yo soy El Centro!—I am The Center!

¡Yo soy el mero mero!—I am the one and only!

DEDICATIONS

In remembrance of my big orange gato, Jambi, and to all my family and friends, here and in the land of Mictlan. **—Cathy Camper**

To Juaritos Lindo, el Noa Noa, JuanGa, y los ciudadanos de El Paso, Tejas. **—Raúl the Third**

ACKNOWLEDGMENTS

¡MUCHAS GRACIAS!—Diana Miranda and Violeta Garza—who read it first!

A big hand to Ana Schmitt and Ferner O. Bodden for La Manopla.

Many thanks to Mat Johnson and the VONA community for help and support.

Thanks to: Matty Monaghan, Omar the buff tiger, Raúl Gonzalez III, Delia Palomeque Morales, Diana Nunez, Byrd, Josh Rodriguez, Lucy Iraola, Mary Conde, Anne Seeman, Cynthia Cowen, Laura Jones, Sara Ryan, Rob Kirby, John Capecci, Amy Sedaris, El Vez, Davy Rothbart, Jon Scieszka, Megan McDonald, David Henry Sterry and Arielle Eckstut (The Book Doctors), Reforma Folks and WOC Zine friends, Roberto Y. Hernandez—your ride is awesome!, Jennifer Laughran, Ginee Seo, Taylor Norman, Neil Egan, Lara Starr, Jaime Wong, Sally Kim, and all the other wonderful people at Chronicle Books, Multnomah County Library staff and resources, my family, and everyone else who believed in and supported this road trip!

Many thanks to *Science Made Stupid*, by Tom Weller, for Flappy's geological knowledge. For more information about this book, go to http://tweller.com/. To read it online: http://www.chrispennello.com/tweller/. **—C. C.**

Thanks to Elaine Bay and Raúl El Gonzalez IV, my two loves!! . . . and to Dave O., Ruben and Danny G., Jennifer Laughran, Question Mark and the Mysterians, every one of my students, Ginee Seo, Taylor Norman, Caleb Neelon, Leo Espinosa, Karen Moss, and Joseph Carroll. Special thanks to my Art Director, Neil Egan, for keeping me on track and putting all the pieces together! **—R**

For a list of sources and works cited, please visit www.chroniclebooks.com/lowridersinspace.

AUTHOR'S NOTE

The Aztec religion was complex and included over two hundred gods. Part of their religion involved human sacrifice, to ensure that the rhythms and cycles of nature and the world would continue undisturbed. If a person died a normal death, it was believed they passed through nine layers of the underworld, including a wind of knives that stripped their flesh from their bones. They continued as skeletons to the land of Mictlan, ruled by Mictlantecuhtli, the Aztec god of the underworld.

The Aztecs had many scientific and technological skills, including astronomy and herbal medicine. They were also skilled stone sculptors, although much is unknown about their stone quarries and their stone carving techniques. Their stone sculptures were mainly carved of igneous rocks like andesite, diorite, and basalt—rocks found in the volcanic countryside where they lived.

Tepeyollotl is the Jaguar god, who rules over animals, darkened caves, echoes, and earthquakes. His spotted coat was supposed to represent the stars in the sky.

Coyote is a trickster who enjoys playing tricks and pranks in both ancient Aztec culture and in the beliefs of native Southwest American people. The Aztec god Huehuecoyotl, whose name means "very old coyote," enjoyed playing tricks too, and was also the god of storytelling, music, dance, and merriment.

Xilonen is the young Aztec goddess of maize, or corn, and fertility, who holds cobs of corn in her hands. In her more mature form, she is known as Chicomecoatl.

La Llorona, or "The Weeping Woman," is a ghostly woman who wanders the Mexican countryside looking for her lost children, and crying out "Ay mis hijos!" ("Oh my children!").

Chupacabra—the goat-sucker—is a monster known throughout Central and South America and the Caribbean. Mysterious incidences of dead livestock are often blamed on Chupacabra, who is thought to look somewhat like a mangy dog with spines down its back and glowing red eyes.

El Cucuy is like the boogeyman in the United States. "El Cucuy will get you if you don't stop that now!" parents might say to get their children to behave. Like the boogeyman, he doesn't have a specific shape, but people imagine him hiding under beds and in dark closets, waiting to pounce.

Lucha Libre means "free fighting" and is the name for professional wrestling in Mexico and other Spanish speaking countries in Central and South America and the Caribbean. Luchadores who wear masks are called *máscara*. They may be *rudos* (bad guys or brawlers) or *técnicos* (good guys, literally technicians). A fight between a masked fighter and an unmasked fighter is called *máscara contra cabellera* ("mask versus hair"). When losing a match, the ultimate humiliation for a masked fighter would be to have his mask removed in public, while, for an unmasked luchador, a loss would result in him having to shave his head.

Mictlantecuhtli, the Aztec god of the underworld, was one of the major Aztec gods. With his wife, Mictecacíhuatl, he ruled the underworld. He's often portrayed as a skeleton, with his liver dangling inside his ribcage, and wearing a skull mask, necklaces of eyeballs, and bone ear plugs. He has curly dark hair and penetrating eyes that allow him to see in the dark. He's associated with spiders, owls, and bats.

Day of the Dead/Día de los Muertos takes place November 1 and 2 and is celebrated in Mexico and many Latin American countries. In this celebration, which goes back to pre-Columbian times, people lovingly remember relatives and friends who have died. Altars, or *ofrendas*, are made in honor of the deceased, and are decorated with marigolds, *papel picados* (tissue paper stencils), sugar skulls, papier-mâché skeletons, foods and drinks the person loved, and, for children, toys they played with. Gravesites are cleaned and decorated, and often families and friends will stay all night in the cemetery visiting with the deceased. Day of the Dead parades feature large crafted skeletons, masks, and people in elaborate skeleton costumes. The parades sometimes lead to cemeteries and are themselves a kind of moving, living altar to those departed and remembered.

This book was written to celebrate the artistry, inventiveness, mechanical aptitude, resilience, and humor that is all a part of lowrider culture. We were also greatly inspired by Aztec art, stories, and the codices which recorded Aztec culture, in creating this graphic novel.

Library of Congress Cataloging-in-Publication Data available.

ISBN 978-1-4521-2343-1 [hardcover]
ISBN 978-1-4521-3836-7 [paperback]

Manufactured in China.

Design by Neil J. Egan III.
Additional typesetting by Liam Flanagan, Lisa Schneller, and Tara Creehan.
Typeset in Comicraft Hedge Backwards, P22 Posada, and ITC Century.

10 9 8 7 6 5 4 3 2 1

Chronicle Books LLC
680 Second Street
San Francisco, CA 94107